Dinosaur Rampage

by **Craig Allen**

Illustrated by **Alek Sotirovski**

Titles in the Full Flight Thrills and Spills series:

The Knight Olympics	Jonny Zucker
Pied Piper of London	Danny Pearson
The Science Project	Jane A C West
Gorilla Thriller	Richard Taylor
Clone Zone	Jillian Powell
Clowning Around	Helen Orme
Time to go Home	David Orme
Haunted Car	Roger Hurn
Dinosaur Rampage	Craig Allen
Rubbish Ghost	Jillian Powell

Badger Publishing Limited

Oldmedow Road, Hardwick Industrial Estate,

King's Lynn PE30 4JJ

Telephone: 01438 791037

www.badgerlearning.co.uk

2 4 6 8 10 9 7 5 3

Dinosaur Rampage ISBN 978-1-84926-993 3

Text © Craig Allen 2013

Complete work © Badger Publishing Limited 2013

Second edition © 2014

Publisher: Susan Ross

Senior Editor: Danny Pearson

Designer: Fiona Grant

Illustrator: Alek Sotirovski

Contents

New words:

exhibit	museum
lightning	dreaming
skeleton	sprinting
fearsome	vegetarian
vanished	stomping

Main characters:

Bronte

Jack

Kaitlin

Chapter 1

Death Valley

"I can't believe I'm up so early,"
said Jack.

"It's only 7 am," replied Kaitlin.

"Yes, but it is Saturday and it is raining,"
said Jack.

Kaitlin and Jack were up early so they
could go and see the new exhibit at the
local museum.

There was a real buzz around the town
about the new dinosaur bones that had
been found.

Two dinosaur skeletons had been discovered in a place called Death Valley. It got that name because people said they had seen ghosts there.

Kaitlin and Jack ran down the street trying to avoid the rain. It was a wet and stormy day.

"Why are we here this early? The museum doesn't open until 9.30," said Jack.

"I want to be the first person in the town to see them," said Kaitlin.

Kaitlin and Jack soon arrived at the museum.

"This had better be good," said Jack.

"Oh, stop moaning," said Kaitlin crossly.

As they waited in the rain, the sky suddenly lit up.

"Wow, look at that," said Jack.

Kaitlin looked up and saw a lightning bolt coming down from the sky.

"Look out!" shouted Kaitlin.

The bolt of lightning crashed down and hit the museum, lighting the whole building up.

Kaitlin and Jack watched in shock.

"I hope it hasn't caused any damage," said Jack.

Before Kaitlin could answer, a loud noise came from inside the museum.

It sounded like stomping.

Kaitlin and Jack looked at each other. The ground moved under their feet as the thudding came nearer.

What was going on?

Suddenly, the side door to the museum flew open and out ran a full-sized stegosaurus skeleton.

"I thought they only found a couple of bones!" shouted Jack.

Seconds later a bigger skeleton crashed out.

It was the skeleton of a fearsome tyrannosaurus-rex.

Both dinosaurs ran towards the woods.

Chapter 2

Steg

"Am I dreaming?" asked Kaitlin.

"I wish," said Jack. "Where did the museum say these dinosaur bones were found?"

"Death Valley," replied Kaitlin.

"That might explain it! We need to tell someone," said Jack.

"It will be too late. Come on, let's chase after them," said Kaitlin.

"No way!" replied Jack.

"Come on, before we lose them," said Kaitlin.

Jack still didn't look sure. Kaitlin grabbed Jack's elbow and started sprinting after the skeletons.

"Let's try and get the dinosaurs back to the museum," shouted Kaitlin. "The museum workers will know what to do."

"I don't think they will," said Jack. "This kind of thing doesn't happen every day."

Kaitlin and Jack ran through the woods, following the dinosaurs' footprints.

All of a sudden they came to a stop.

"Where have they gone?" asked Jack.

"Don't move," said Kaitlin, pointing behind Jack.

He spun round and saw the stegosaurus skeleton towering over him.

Kaitlin and Jack stood still as the skeleton dinosaur moved its skull closer to them.

Jack started to turn away, he was terrified.

"Wait, remember what we got told in class?" said Kaitlin. "I don't think it wants to eat us, it's a vegetarian," said Kaitlin.

Kaitlin held out a hand slowly, with one eye closed. The stegosaurus skeleton let her stroke it on the head.

"You see," said Kaitlin, with both eyes open again.

"It's the t-rex I'm worried about," said Jack, still afraid. "They were definitely not vegetarian."

"I'm going to call you Steg," said Kaitlin to the stegosaurus.

As Kaitlin and Jack stood watching the dinosaur skeleton, Kaitlin heard a familiar noise.

"Woof!"

It was Bronte, Kaitlin's dog.

"What are you doing here?" asked Kaitlin.

Kaitlin was pleased to see Bronte but the same couldn't be said for Steg.

When Steg saw Bronte, it was scared and ran away.

Bronte chased Steg through the trees and soon both of them had vanished.

Chapter 3

The Chase

"Why did Bronte chase Steg?" asked Kaitlin.

"It's not every day that Bronte comes face to face with a walking dog treat," said Jack.

Kaitlin looked at him, confused.

"You know, the bones," said Jack. "Should we run after them?"

But as Kaitlin and Jack were wondering what to do next, the noise of a tree crashing to the ground could be heard nearby.

"What was that?" asked Kaitlin.

"I have an idea but I really hope I'm wrong," said Jack.

Kaitlin and Jack looked ahead to where the noise was coming from, and suddenly the huge head of the t-rex skeleton smashed through the trees. It showed its razor-sharp teeth and then charged straight at them.

"It's Rex. Run!" yelled Jack.

Jack and Kaitlin ran through the trees.
Rex was close behind.

"Where are we going?" asked Kaitlin.

"Under here," said Jack, pointing to a small bridge.

Jack and Kaitlin dived under the bridge and sat quietly as they listened to hear where Rex was.

They could hear heavy footsteps getting closer and closer, and then they stopped right above them.

Kaitlin and Jack sat in terror as they listened to what sounded like heavy breathing from above. The t-rex's head was only a few inches away from seeing them.

But then it snorted and stomped off in the other direction.

"Phew," said Kaitlin.

"Are you two OK?" called out a voice.

Chapter 4

Go Fetch!

Kaitlin and Jack looked up and saw their science teacher, Mr Turner.

"Yes sir, thanks," said Kaitlin. "But what are you doing here sir?"

"I was out for a walk in the woods when I saw that massive dinosaur skeleton chasing you both. I couldn't believe what I was seeing, so I ran after you," said Mr Turner. "What on earth is going on?"

"I'll explain," said Kaitlin. She told him everything that had happened to them that morning.

When she'd finished talking, Mr Turner said, "We need to get those two dinosaur skeletons back into the museum. If the lightning did this to them, then maybe lightning can change them back."

"That sounds like a good plan, but how are we going to do that?" asked Jack.

"I don't know," said Mr Turner, "but we need to move quickly before someone gets hurt."

As the trio started to walk off, Kaitlin heard Bronte barking. A plan suddenly popped into her head.

"I know how to get the skeletons back to the museum," she said.

"How?" asked Jack.

"Just trust me, get back to the museum and be sure to bring me some lightning!" yelled Kaitlin as she disappeared into the woods.

Jack stood and stared.

"I hope she knows what she's doing," said Mr Turner.

Kaitlin spotted Bronte in the woods and she ran towards him. As she sat stroking Bronte, Steg appeared.

Steg didn't see them so it didn't run, but Steg didn't see Rex sneaking up behind either. Kaitlin looked at Bronte and told him the plan. Bronte dived under a bush.

Rex crashed forwards and saw Kaitlin. It started to stomp towards her.

But Bronte jumped out from the bush and ran straight for it.

Chapter 5

Now!

As soon as Rex saw Bronte, it turned and ran, and so did Steg. In a few seconds, Bronte was chasing both dinosaurs out of the woods.

Bronte, Steg and Rex crashed through the trees with Kaitlin right behind.

They soon arrived back at the museum. Rex and Steg ran straight for the museum's back door and smashed it open.

Kaitlin watched as Steg, Rex and Bronte ran through the back door, just as Jack and Mr Turner were climbing up a drainpipe and onto the roof.

Kaitlin ran inside the museum and saw that Bronte had chased Steg and Rex back into their display cases. But the skeletons were still alive.

She called to Bronte to join her.

Kaitlin looked up and saw Jack and Mr Turner on the roof, through a large ceiling window that Jack had flung open.

"Whatever you're doing, do it quickly," yelled Kaitlin, "or it will be too late." Steg and Rex were both now growling in their display cases.

"GET ON WITH IT!" shouted Kaitlin.

Up on the roof, Mr Turner had put on some plastic gloves and had found an old metal pole. He held it up in the air and dangled some wire from it through the ceiling window. Five seconds later, a flash of lightning lit up the sky.

The lightning hit the metal pole and shot through the wire into the museum.

The museum lit up just like before.
Mr Turner was thrown off the roof.

Kaitlin watched from inside as the skeletons gave one last roar; then they became still.

Kaitlin and Bronte ran outside to see Jack and Mr Turner.

Jack was climbing back down the drainpipe. He jumped down. Jack, Kaitlin and Bronte ran over to help Mr Turner out from the bush he'd fallen into.

His hair was sticking up!

"Are you OK sir?" asked Kaitlin.

"Yes, I am fine now. Come on, let's get out of here," replied Mr Turner.

Kaitlin, Jack and Mr Turner left the museum before anyone saw them.

Somehow, against the odds, they had saved the town from a dino rampage.

When the museum workers got to the museum that morning, they had no idea why the back door had been smashed in and the large ceiling window was wide open.

Dinosaur Facts

Did you know that there were over 500 species of dinosaur?

A person who studies dinosaurs is known as a palaeontologist.

Most UK dinosaur fossils were found in southern England.

So far, the bones of 108 types of dinosaur have been discovered in the UK.

The first dinosaurs lived 230 million years ago.

The word dinosaur means 'terrible lizard'.

Dinosaurs were the largest land animals of all time and their bones have been discovered in all continents.

The longest dinosaur was seismosaurus, which measured over 40 metres; as long as five double-decker buses.

What killed the dinosaurs?

It is thought that the dinosaurs became extinct due to two massive, destructive events.

The first may have been a meteorite smashing into the Earth.

The second may have been a massive volcano exploding, which caused the whole environment to change.

The dinosaurs became extinct over 65 million years ago.

Questions about the Story

What was the weather like when Kaitlin and Jack got to the museum?

Where were the bones found?

How many dinosaurs came back to life?

What was the name of Kaitlin's dog?

What subject did Mr Turner teach?

What names did Kaitlin and Jack give to the dinosaurs?

How did Kaitlin get the skeletons back to the museum?

What happened when Mr Turner held up the metal pole?